TOURIST TORMENT

SIT, STAY, SLEEP COZY MYSTERIES
BOOK 12

PATTI BENNING

SUMMER PRESCOTT BOOKS PUBLISHING

Copyright 2025 Summer Prescott Books

All Rights Reserved. No part of this publication nor any of the information herein may be quoted from, nor reproduced, in any form, including but not limited to: printing, scanning, photocopying, or any other printed, digital, or audio formats, without prior express written consent of the copyright holder.

**This book is a work of fiction. Any similarities to persons, living or dead, places of business, or situations past or present, is completely unintentional.

CHAPTER ONE

What was once an oasis of quiet had devolved into pure chaos. The din of barking dogs faded behind Sadie Barton as the door to the kennels swung shut behind her, only to be replaced with excited chatter from the people milling in the motel's small lobby.

Penelope Montgomery, whose red hair, usually impeccably groomed, was now a frizzy mess around her head, was trying to talk on the phone while frantically signaling the people in line at the front desk to wait. When she spotted Sadie, her expression changed to one of pure relief, and she waved her over, cupping one hand to the phone's speaker so she could talk.

"Can you take over for a second? I'm trying to deal with the power company. They're saying we didn't pay last month's bill, but I know for a fact we did."

Penny's scowl told Sadie exactly how she felt about this record-keeping mishap from the power company. Glad her friend was the one dealing with it, she nodded and took her place behind the front desk while Penny retreated to the far corner of the room, where the relative quiet would let her concentrate on her phone call in peace.

Sadie smiled at the irritated looking man who was next in line. He had thick, wavy black hair, a roman nose, and wore a pair of chunky rectangular glasses through which he squinted at her.

"Sorry for the wait, sir," she said. "How can I help you?"

"I made a reservation last week," he said. "One adult and one dog, under the name Bryan Parks."

Sadie realized he was holding a leash and leaned forward to peer over the edge of the front desk. A tri-color Australian Shepherd was huddled against the heavy wood desk. The dog looked up at her with wide, stressed eyed, and her short tail was pressed between her legs. She hadn't even noticed the dog when she came into the lobby; the poor thing was practically frozen in fear at all the commotion.

"Oh, I'm sorry, sweetie," she murmured to the

dog. "We'll get you checked in in no time at all. What's her name? Or is she a he?"

"It's a girl," Bryan said. "Do you really need to know the dog's name to check me in? Can I just get the room key?"

Taken aback by the man's irritated answer, Sadie mumbled an apology and pulled up the reservation on Penny's old laptop, which they used as their main work computer. "Yep, I see you in our system. You're staying until Sunday?" He nodded once, wordlessly. Sadie continued; "All right, it looks like you've already paid and we have a card on file, so all I'll need is your ID."

Bryan reached into his pocket and withdrew from his wallet a folded piece of paper. "All I have is a temporary driver's license," he said. "I lost mine a couple weeks ago, and I'm still waiting for the replacement in the mail. Is this enough? I figured if it's good enough to drive with, it should be good enough to rent a motel room with."

Sadie took the paper and unfolded it. She hadn't seen a temporary driver's license in years, not since a dog at her first job chewed her license up and she had to get one herself from the Kentucky DMV. Everything seemed to be in order, so she recorded his driver's license number and handed the paper back to him.

"That'll be fine," she assured him. "Normally, we like having a photo ID, but since you already have a credit card on file, I'll count that as a second form of ID. Here's your key; you'll be in Room Four. I hope you and your dog have a pleasant stay."

He accepted the key and left without another word to her. His poor dog was so frightened that he practically had to drag her behind him. Sadie hoped the poor thing got a chance to relax a little once she was in the peace and quiet of the motel room. She felt worse about making the dog wait than the man; Bryan Parks had been rude. A simple "thank you" would have gone a long way.

She turned her attention to the next guests; a group of three young people who looked like they were in their early twenties. The two young men were laughing at a video on one of their phones, but the young woman noticed they were up and stepped forward. After shooting her companions an exasperated look, she took her ID out of her slender wallet and set it down in front of Sadie.

"We have a reservation for two rooms under Kelsey Marloe," she said. Turning, she raised her voice at the two young men. "Neil, Rory, stop watching that stupid video. They might need your IDs too."

"Hey, maybe she'll know something." The blond haired young man nudged his companion, who had auburn hair drawn back into a small bun, who nodded in agreement and approached to hold his phone out to Sadie.

"Have you seen this video?"

He hit play, and Sadie found herself watching a short, blurry clip of a reddish brown creature moving through the trees. It was only briefly visible before vanishing into the undergrowth.

"No, I can't say I have," Sadie said. "What is it? A bear?"

"No," the man said, sounding almost offended. "It's a skunk ape! The video was taken in the forest around Greencreek a couple years ago."

"What's a skunk ape?" she asked. She had the feeling that she was about to be the butt of a joke, but she couldn't help but bite. Her eyes narrowed. "Is it like bigfoot?"

"Yes," the auburn haired man said in the same instant the blond haired man said, "*No.*" They glared at each other for a second before the auburn hair man turned back to her.

"Ignore Rory, he's an amateur. *Professionals*

believe the skunk ape is either another name for bigfoot, or a closely related subspecies endemic to the swamps of the southeastern United States. Most people aren't aware of this, but there's an underground cave network spanning the country that's thought to be where these creatures spend most of their time, which explains why they're so elusive."

"Neil, you're boring the poor woman to death," Kelsey said. Turning back to Sadie, she added. "Ignore both of them. They'll talk your ear off about cryptids if you let them. We *are* here to see if we can figure out what that video captured, but we don't all think it's a mythological animal. Personally, I think it's a black bear with a rare color mutation."

"She's the skeptic of our team," Neil chimed in.

"And the only one who can actually organize something like this," Rory muttered. "For what it's worth, *I* believe skunk apes are a completely different phenomenon to bigfoot–"

"Oh my gosh," Kelsey groaned. "Can we just finish checking in? I need a break from these guys before they drive me insane."

Amused, Sadie recorded the information on Kelsey's driver's license and passed out the keys for Rooms Six and Seven. Once the three of them left, the lobby was empty again, except for Penny. Her friend looked like she was just tying things up on the phone. Sadie could tell by her expression that the issue had resolved in her favor. Good; the last thing they needed right now was a crisis.

It was officially summer, which was, in Sadie's opinion, the worst of Georgia's four seasons. But the hot, humid weather, paired with the fact that a good chunk of the population had time off from school, meant that it was becoming one of their busiest months yet. They hadn't been here for a full year, which meant this was their first June, and they were getting a lot more backpackers, hikers, and people simply traveling through than either of them had expected.

All eight kennels were occupied by boarding dogs, and Sadie had been forced to move Jasper and Angus upstairs to her apartment. She was glad they had each other for company, because for the next week or so, their lives were going to be pretty boring. She was trying to go up there as often as possible to check on them and spend a few minutes training them or just petting them, but for the past week it seemed like she always had something pressing on her plate — and this weekend wasn't going to be any different.

Their motel rooms were fully booked as well, and as a result, their business was doing great. But with just the two of them and two part-time employees — one, a housekeeper who only came by twice a week — it meant that she and Penny barely got a spare moment to breathe.

The one bright spot she was looking forward to today was the Level 2 Obedience class she was hosting tonight. Not only did she love her classes because it meant she got to spend a dedicated hour working directly with dogs and their owners and got to see how much they had improved since last week's class, but her boyfriend, Sam, was also attending tonight's class with his big redbone coonhound named Briar.

Briar was a good dog, but he had spent most of his life running amok with his sister, both of them with free access to his previous owner's acreage and very little in the way of discipline or rules. He and Sam had passed her Level 1 Obedience class a couple of weeks ago, and his behavior was already night-and-day different than it had been when Sam first adopted him.

She was looking forward to seeing his progress, but mostly, she was looking forward to seeing Sam. They hadn't been able to see each other as much as usual this past week, since he was busy with his lawn care business and she had been busy with the motel, so it would be a nice chance to spend some time together, even if she would be busy working with other clients at the same time.

Penny ended the call and leaned back in her seat with a groan. "Finally. I can't believe I spent half an hour on the phone just because someone on their end forgot to record the payment properly."

"At least it's all sorted out now," Sadie said. "Do you want to take a break? I can spend twenty or thirty minutes in here. The dog shouldn't need anything else for a while. I will have to go start getting set up for my class soon, though."

"I might take like five minutes to go make some tea in my room," Penny said. "Do you want some?"

"Sure. Tea sounds good."

Penny got up, but before she reached the door, it opened. This time, it wasn't a guest who came in. The newcomer was Hunter Underwood, the young man who made deliveries for Sunshine Desserts, the local cookie shop. He held two white cardboard boxes that Sadie knew were full of Bailey's famous cookies, and she rushed to hold the door for him so he wouldn't have to risk dropping them as he came in.

"Thanks," he said cheerfully as he walked inside and set the boxes down on the front desk. He set a piece of paper down on top — their invoice, Sadie knew. Thankfully, they were doing well enough that they no longer struggled to pay their basic expenses. It was slow going, but the motel's finances *were* improving.

"Your parking lot is packed," he said. "I had to block some people in, so I better not stick around for long. Loretta must be getting your overflow guests."

"Hold on, Loretta has guests?" Penny asked from where she had been peeking into the top box of cookies. They got a random assortment of both dog and human cookies a few times a week, and they always liked seeing what new flavors Bailey had added.

"Yeah, a couple on their honeymoon," Hunter said. "She stopped in this morning to pick up some complimentary cookies for them."

Penny scowled. "She's giving away the cookies for free? We can't do that, not yet."

Hunter grinned. "Don't worry, I don't think she's about to run you out of business," he said. "Bailey says she's glad for her. Apparently, she hasn't had guests in years. I didn't even know that old bed and breakfast was still running until a couple of weeks ago."

"Yeah, we heard her business took a turn for the worse after her son passed away," Sadie said.

Penny winced. "Right, I forgot about that. Poor

woman. I guess it *is* good that she's doing better now."

"We're trying to get her on the same regular delivery plan you guys are on, but it sounds like she isn't quite ready for that yet," Hunter said. "As far as I'm concerned, the more people who want cookies, the better. Oh, and while I'm catching you up on all the major news, guess who's been hanging around the cookie shop recently?"

"I have no idea," Sadie said, amused. As a delivery driver for one of the most popular businesses in town, Hunter never had a shortage of gossip to share.

"Calvin Deering," he said.

"He's Brian Deering's nephew, right?" Sadie said. She remembered the kind and lonely older man, who had been tragically murdered a few months ago. He had a sweet, elderly beagle who Norma Underwood, Hunter's great-aunt, had adopted.

"That's right," Hunter said.

"I didn't even know he was still in town," Penny said. "He inherited his uncle's house, right?"

"Yeah, and I guess he decided to stay in town. For the past week, he's been coming to Sunshine Desserts every day. I suspect he's just coming in to talk to Bailey; I don't think he's even eating most of the cookies he buys. I'm pretty sure I saw him handing a few off to random passersby after he left the shop."

"Well, that would be an interesting match," Penny said, sounding amused.

They didn't know Calvin Deering well, but from what Sadie remembered of him, he was a rather serious man in his late twenties or early thirties, who was already balding and seemed as if he was perpetually annoyed at everyone. It was hard to imagine him and cheerful, energetic Bailey together.

"What about you?" Penny asked, drawing Sadie out of her thoughts. "Are you and Tanisha still talking?"

"We've been keeping in touch," Hunter said. Someone honked outside and he glanced toward the door. "I'd better go move my van. I'll see you guys Saturday."

He raised a hand in farewell and hurried out the door. Penny looked amused as she left to go make tea, and Sadie smiled a little as she settled back down behind the front desk. It seemed love was brewing in Greencreek.

CHAPTER TWO

Friday morning, Sadie woke up feeling well-rested and ready for whatever the busy day ahead might bring. Her Level Two Obedience class had gone phenomenally well, and she had spent a pleasant evening afterward with Sam, first making and then eating dinner together at his house while the dogs napped on the living room rug.

It seemed she was the only one who had gotten decent sleep, though, because when she went down to the lobby to check on the boarding dogs and begin her kennel chores, Penny was already up and slouched over the front desk..

"You're up early," Sadie said after her initial startle. "Everything all right?"

"No," her friend grumbled. "That dog in Room

Four kept me up half the night, barking. I think its owner left it alone, because I knocked on the door around midnight, but no one answered. It finally settled down a little after one but was at it again early this morning."

"Her owner must have been out late," Sadie said. "He might not even realize the dog was barking. I'll give him a call and let him know. I wish we could offer day care, but we're full up on overnight boarding clients right now."

They needed more kennels, but a major expansion would be expensive. On the other hand, with more kennel space, they might be able to pay a loan off quickly...

"Well, hopefully the dog's owner stays in tonight. I need my beauty sleep." She groaned. "I can feel a headache coming on. I'm going to go grab some painkillers and drink another cup of coffee before I start my day."

Sadie patted her friend's shoulder as she passed, then took her seat at the front desk, where she picked up the old landline that was connected to the room phones. She dialed the extension for Room Four, wanting to let the Australian Shepherd's owner know that his dog had been barking all night before he had a chance to leave for the day. She assumed that he would be in, given the early hour, but the room phone rang for a good two minutes straight before she finally settled the old phone back in its cradle.

No answer, but maybe he was in the shower, or perhaps he was simply a deep sleeper. She decided to try again soon and got up to go take care of the boarding dogs — only to get interrupted yet again when the lobby door opened and a middle-aged woman, whom Sadie recognized as one of their guests, came in.

"Good morning," Sadie said, straightening her scrubs self-consciously. They were the best thing to wear while she was taking care of the dogs and cleaning kennels, but she was aware they weren't exactly flattering on her and probably weren't the most professional thing to wear while taking care of the motel side of the business. "How can I help you, ma'am?"

"I wanted to let you know that one of the other guests has a barking dog who kept me up half the night, and I can't have been the only one who was being bothered by it. I'm in Room Five, and it sounded like it was right next to me. I know dogs can't be expected to be completely silent, but this was excessive."

"Thanks for letting me know," Sadie said. "We're

aware of the situation, and I'm going to give the owner a chance to resolve it before we take any other action. I haven't been able to reach him yet, but as soon as I do, I'll let him know that it can't happen again."

"Well, at least you're on top of it," the woman said. "What about those three hooligans? Are you going to give them a talking to as well?"

"I'm sorry," Sadie said. "Hooligans?"

"Two young men and one young woman, all around the same age," the woman said. "They were loud all evening yesterday, laughing and shouting and playing music late into the night. And this morning, when I got up to take a quick walk around the property, I saw a bunch of garbage spread across the grassy area next to the motel. I can only imagine they're the ones behind it."

Sadie's mind immediately flashed to Neil, Rory, and Kelsey, the three young people who had come to search for the mysterious skunk ape. She could see the two young men being rowdy, but Kelsey seemed like the type who would try to keep them in line. She could be wrong, though — all she had to go off of was a couple minutes' conversation while she was checking them in.

"Let me go see what's going on," she said. "Can you show me where you found the garbage?"

The woman nodded, and Sadie followed her out of the motel. She couldn't spot anything from out front, but the woman led her down the row of rooms, and as soon as they rounded the far corner of the building, she saw what looked like an entire bag of garbage scattered across the grass. All she could do for a few seconds was blink and stare.

Had an animal gotten into their dumpster last night? She couldn't imagine why on earth a person would do something like this, but she also wasn't sure what sort of animal could carry a full garbage bag out of their closed dumpster, all the way across the parking lot, and onto the grass next to the motel. She didn't think a raccoon would even be able to get into the dumpster, let alone drag a garbage bag out of it. Had it been a bear?

Her expression fell into a scowl as she considered something else. Was one of the cryptid hunters behind this, after all, hoping to blame the mess on their skunk ape? The more she thought about it, the more it made sense; maybe one of them wanted to prank the others. It might be all in good fun, but it left her with quite the mess to clean up.

"See?" the woman said. "It's a disgusting mess. I

know this wasn't here yesterday. You have a lovely motel, hon, but I think you need to be a little more careful about who you let stay here."

"Thanks for bringing this to my attention," Sadie said. "I'll get this cleaned up as soon as possible, and if you'd like, I can issue a partial refund for last night's stay, since your sleep was interrupted by the barking dog."

She wasn't going to address the other part of the woman's comment. They weren't about to start turning guests away willy-nilly — she didn't want to turn *anyone* away unless they were clearly a danger to themselves or others — but she could understand the woman's frustration. No one wanted to stay at a motel that was surrounded by garbage.

The woman's expression grew much more pleasant. "Oh, would you? I'd appreciate that. Thank you so much."

"Of course. If you want to stop back into the lobby later today, either myself or Penny will take care of that. Right now, I need to start cleaning this up."

She also still had to let the dogs out, so she hurried back into the lobby and then through the laundry room and into the kennel room to do that first. She took Jasper and Angus out on their leashes, then hurried them back upstairs before going *back* down to get a couple of big black garbage bags from the laundry room. She ran into Penny on her way out and had to explain what was going on while they walked down the row of rooms to the far side of the motel. Penny looked livid when she saw the garbage.

"What is wrong with people?" she complained as she began helping Sadie pick up the trash. "I can't believe someone would do this. It's just so... so *rude*."

"I thought it might be an animal," Sadie said, pausing to examine a stained piece of mail. "But I don't think this came from our dumpster. It looks like it might be from behind the diner."

"That explains why there's so much food trash," Penny muttered. "Who would go through all the effort of getting a bag of garbage from the diner and bringing it here?"

"Someone who didn't want to be caught on the security cameras," Sadie replied, turning to look at the motel. None of the security cameras were looking out over this area, which meant that if someone pulled up along the road, they would have been able to make this mess without having to worry about being recorded.

"But why?" Penny said as she threw away a rotten

banana peel. She wrinkled her nose. "There's no point unless they want to upset us. In that case, I'd say it's working."

Sadie was about to tell Penny her theory about one of the adventurous trio being behind the garbage spill in an effort to blame it on the skunk ape when something caught her eye — it wasn't a normal piece of trash, but what looked like a perfectly good cell phone lying in the grass, a few feet away from the bulk of the mess.

She stooped to grab it, and to her surprise, the screen came to life when she pressed the button on the side.

"What did you find?" her friend asked, coming over to look at it with her.

"I think this belongs to one of our guests," Sadie muttered, frowning at the phone's background. It was a picture of a very familiar-looking Australian Shepherd; Ivy, the dog in Room Four… the same dog that had kept Penny and at least one guest up half the night with her barking.

Sadie looked from the phone back to the garbage, more confused than ever. Was the Australian Shepherd's grumpy owner the one behind this? That made even less sense than this being part of a fake skunk ape sighting. He seemed like a no-nonsense sort of individual, not someone who would cut open a garbage bag and fling the contents all over the grass without a very good reason.

"If it belongs to one of our guests, then that's proof, right?" Penny said. "They must have dropped it when they did this."

"Let's find out," Sadie said.

She pocketed the phone and, leaving her half-full garbage bag on the ground, marched back along the row of rooms until she reached Room Four, where she knocked on the door. From inside, she heard the dog begin barking and saw the curtains move as a curious black, brown, and white face investigated her from the window. She knocked again, but there was no response besides barking.

"I'll go get the master key," Penny said.

"Will you get one of the slip leads from the kennel, too?" she called out after her.

Sadie tried to calm the dog down through the door while Penny raced back to the lobby, but the Australian Shepherd was frantic, barking and whining as she jumped at the door and the window. It was a relief when Penny returned, with the key and slip lead in hand.

She handed the latter to Sadie and unlocked the door before stepping back to let Sadie crack it open and loop the leash over the dog's head as she tried to dart out. As soon as the lead drew taut, the dog tucked her tail between her legs and crouched low to the ground, giving Sadie a mournful, frightened look.

"It's all right, sweetie," she said softly. "We're just here to figure out what's going on, that's all."

"Eww," Penny said, wrinkling her nose. "How long has she been alone? She had a couple accidents."

Sadie peered into the room and saw that her friend was right. The dog had left a couple messes on the carpet, but other than that, the room looked untouched. Penny walked in further, checking the drawers and then the bathroom.

"There's nothing in here," she said as she returned to Sadie. "Not even a water bowl."

"Poor girl."

She crouched to make herself look smaller and, not looking directly at the dog, made kissing noises and snapped her fingers quietly. Ever so slowly, the frightened dog crept closer to her until she was huddled up right against Sadie's bent legs. Sadie scratched her behind the ears and after a few seconds, the dog began to relax. She laid down on her side, and her stubby tail began to wag.

"That's it," Sadie said quietly. "I'm not so scary,

am I? Let's go get you some water and see if we can track down your owner."

She was upset but tried not to show it for the dog's sake. There was no point in being angry yet, not until she knew what happened. She didn't want to assume bad intentions if it turned out the dog's owner had gotten into a car accident or ended up in the hospital unexpectedly. For now, she would make sure the dog was safe and hydrated, and then she and Penny would get to the bottom of this mystery.

CHAPTER THREE

Sadie kept a dog bowl filled with fresh water in the lobby, and as soon as they entered the building, Ivy rushed over to it and began to gulp the water down. The urgency with which she drank made Sadie suspect she hadn't had water all night; possibly not since she and her owner checked in yesterday.

Once the dog was satisfied, Sadie sat on one of the uncomfortable chairs against the far wall – they really should just get rid of them, none of the guests ever used them – and gently felt the dog over, then checked her gums for color to make sure she wasn't injured or sick. Satisfied that, other than being a bit dehydrated, Ivy seemed to be in good health, she tied the dog to the laundry room door handle: not ideal, but the position allowed Ivy to reach the dog bed and the water bowl while being restrained in case someone opened the lobby door.

As the dog occupied herself with one of Jasper's toys, Sadie joined Penny behind the front desk. Her friend had already pulled up the security camera footage and had found the recording from when Bryan Parks checked in yesterday. Sadie watched as he and Ivy walked into the lobby. Twenty minutes later, he walked out again with Ivy by his side and went directly to Room Four. She saw him unlock the door, peer inside, then unclip the dog's leash and shove her into the room before shutting and locking the door.

Then he got into his vehicle and drove away.

"He's driving a silver convertible," Penny murmured. "I'm going to go through the rest of the footage quickly to see if he comes back at all."

She watched as Penny checked the parking lot's footage, but unless it was in a clip they missed, Bryan didn't return, not even once. Poor Ivy had been alone in the room with no food or water for almost eighteen hours.

"I'm so sorry, girl," Sadie said, turning to look at the dog.

She felt a surge of guilt at the thought that she had been going about her day, feeding and petting and playing with all the other dogs, while poor Ivy was alone in the motel room, hungry and thirsty and scared.

"I'm going to call the sheriff," Penny said. "This has to be illegal."

"I don't know if it counts as abandonment since he hasn't been gone for twenty-four hours yet, but go ahead," Sadie said. "I don't know what to do with Ivy if he doesn't come back soon; we don't have space in the kennels, and I don't want to put her upstairs with Jasper and Angus. They're both good dogs, but she's a stranger and I don't know whether they'll get along."

She walked over to Ivy, who immediately dropped the toy and looked up at her, wagging her stubby tail rapidly. She petted the dog while she tried to figure out what the next steps were if Sheriff Islington couldn't locate Ivy's owner. Maybe she could set a crate up for Ivy right here in the lobby. That way, she and Penny could keep an eye on her throughout the day. Then, at night, she could bring the crate upstairs to her apartment. It would be a pain to carry the big, wire crate up the stairs, but it seemed like the smartest and safest option for everyone.

At least her owner had attached a vaccination record when he emailed them to make the reservation, so she could be relatively sure that Ivy wasn't carrying any illnesses that could spread to Jasper and Angus.

"He says he'll be here in about twenty minutes," Penny said as she put her phone down. "Do you want me to watch her while you take care of the dogs? I know your mornings are usually pretty busy."

"Sure, thanks," Sadie said, straightening up. "She might have to go outside soon, since she just drank all that water. Oh, and feel free to give her one of the dog cookies from Sunshine Desserts. She's probably hungry, and those are usually pretty gentle on the dogs' stomachs."

Penny nodded and came over to introduce herself to the dog. Sadie waited until they seemed comfortable together, then went into the kennel room to begin her daily cleaning chores and feed all of the boarding dogs who were clamoring for their late breakfast.

By the time Penny texted her to let her know Sheriff Islington had arrived, Sadie's scrubs were soaking wet from the knees down due to a mishap with the hose she used to disinfect the kennels, and she felt like a grimy mess, but this was urgent so she would just have to go out there as she was. She shut the hose off, double-checked that all the kennels were latched, and returned to the lobby, where Penny and the sheriff were waiting for her.

Penny was holding Ivy's leash, and the dog sat pressed against the backs of her legs, peering around her at the sheriff, whose tall form and broad-brimmed hat seemed to intimidate her.

"Hey," Penny said, glancing over her shoulder. "Cody got here a couple minutes ago; I told him what's going on, then I sent him to clean the messes in Room Four."

"Poor guy," Sadie said, her lips twitching.

Better him than her – she cleaned up enough dog messes as it was, and he had known that cleaning the rooms and picking up after dogs were both in his job description when they hired him. He probably didn't expect to have to do both at once, but someone had to do it, and he had drawn the short straw.

"It's been a while since I've had to respond to a call from you guys," Sheriff Islington said, giving her a nod in greeting. "Penny said you have an abandoned dog."

"We think she's abandoned," Sadie said. "Her owner dropped her off yesterday afternoon and hasn't been back since. She was left in the motel room with nothing, not even a bowl of water, and no one came to let her out either, so she left messes on the floor."

"Did you happen to get a photo of the room's condition before you sent your employee to clean up?"

Sadie's stomach sank, but to her relief, Penny nodded. "I asked Cody to take some pictures and text them to me in case we needed evidence."

"We aren't one hundred percent sure she was abandoned," Sadie said. She didn't like to think that someone could have left their dog behind on purpose without even a bowl of water. "It's possible her owner got into an accident or had some sort of medical emergency and couldn't come back for her."

"Have you tried calling him?" Sheriff Islington said.

Sadie shook her head. "No. But only because we found his phone in the grass outside, and his cell is the only number we have for him."

"Shoot, I completely forgot about that mess," Penny muttered. At Sheriff Islington's raised eyebrow, she explained about the torn-open garbage bag that seemed to have come all the way from the diner's dumpster in town — and the cell phone with a picture of Ivy on it, which had been laying on the ground nearby.

"I see," the sheriff drawled. "So, our suspect rented a room… for how long?"

TOURIST TORMENT   31

"He arrived Thursday afternoon, and was supposed to check out on Sunday," Sadie replied.

"He rents a motel room for three nights, only to abandon his dog day one, commit an act of petty vandalism, and flee, accidentally leaving his cell phone behind." He tugged on his goatee. "It seems like our suspect might be having a mental crisis."

"What should we do?" Penny asked. "I mean, I think we're both upset about the vandalism, but that doesn't really matter compared to him leaving his dog behind."

"I'll try to track down his next of kin and see if we can figure out what's going on," Sheriff Islington said. "Do you have space to keep the dog here for now?"

"No," Sadie said. She was reluctant to admit it, but it just wasn't ideal, especially if Ivy was going to be here for days.

The sheriff didn't seem to hear her, turning his attention instead to his pocket, where his phone was buzzing incessantly.

"One second," he said. He answered the call and turned away as he pressed the phone to his ear. Penny and Sadie both waited as he listened to whatever the person on the other end was saying, then ended the call with a "Yep, be right there," before turning back around to face them. "One of you text me the guest's information — whatever you have on him. I need to run." He paused, then added, "Oh, you can place that border collie if you want. I heard back from the estate lawyer; the family just wants him to be placed in a good home."

"Wait, what's going on?" Penny called out after him.

He paused at the lobby door and looked back at her. "Sunshine Desserts is on fire."

CHAPTER FOUR

Sheriff Islington was out the door in a flash, with no time for their questions. Sadie exchanged a look with her best friend.

Penny mouthed, *What?*

Sadie got over her shock enough to say, "Is there something in the water? Why is the entire town going insane today?"

"I hope Bailey's okay," her friend said, clutching Ivy's leash tighter. "One of us should go and see what's going on."

"I'll take care of things here if you want to go," Sadie offered.

Penny looked tempted, but after a second, she shook her head. "As much as I want to, you should go. You know Bailey better than I do, and who knows what state the cookie shop is in. She might need a friendly face."

"All right, I'll let you know what's going on when I get there. What about Ivy?"

"I'll keep her up here with me for now," Penny said. "She seems like a quiet dog, and the company will be nice. Just keep me in the loop, okay? I'll let you know if her owner comes back."

"Thanks," Sadie said. She grabbed her purse from behind the front desk, paused to scratch Ivy under the chin, and then hurried out the door.

As soon as she safely navigated out of the busy parking lot with her SUV, she raced toward town. She could see the smoke before she even got there. It rose in dark plumes above the main road, which was already blocked off by fire trucks and first responders. Sadie parked along the curb a good distance down the block and got out of her vehicle to join the crowd of bystanders.

She spotted a familiar silhouette as she drew closer and called out Sam's name as she jogged over to join him. He had managed to get a spot right at the front of the crowd and made room for her as she approached. He had a takeout bag from the diner clutched in one hand; he must have stopped for breakfast on his way to or from one of his landscaping jobs.

"What's going on?" she asked.

He pulled his phone out of his pocket to type his response; it wasn't his favorite way to talk, but it was the easiest, especially when he only had one hand free.

No idea. I was in the diner when the building started smoking. Firefighters arrived just a few minutes later.

"Sheriff Islington was at the motel when he got the call," Sadie said. "I followed him here; Penny and I wanted to see what was going on and make sure Bailey is okay."

In response, Sam nodded across the road. Sadie followed his gaze and saw Bailey and Hunter huddled together with Norma Underwood, who owned the hardware store just down the road. Norma spotted her looking and waved. When Bailey followed her look and saw Sadie, she gestured her over. Sadie and Sam hurried across the road to join them.

"If you came into town for cookies, you're out of luck," Bailey said with forced sarcasm. She looked shaken and smelled strongly of smoke but seemed otherwise unharmed.

"Sheriff Islington shared the news with us," Sadie said. "What happened?"

"I don't know yet. I was out front, rearranging the cookie displays, when I smelled smoke. Someone must have spilled some oil or something, because some sort of liquid was creeping under the back door… and it was on fire. I screamed at Hunter to call 911 and got both of us out of there, then started letting my neighbors know what was going on so they could evacuate too. No one's hurt, and I don't think the damage to the cookie shop is too bad, but it was a close call. If it had happened when we weren't there…" She shuddered. "I don't know how bad it could have been."

"I'm telling you, it was those three troublemakers," Norma said. "They were being utterly obnoxious when they came into the hardware store, and I'm almost certain they're the ones who vandalized the alley behind the shops this morning – someone left all sorts of rude graffiti. They frightened Mulberry when one of them put on a horrible bigfoot mask, and I had to shout at them to get out."

"I don't know," Bailey said. "They stopped in earlier, and they seemed fine to me."

"Hold on. Three troublemakers?" Sadie asked. The mention of a bigfoot mask – knowing them, it was probably supposed to be a skunk ape – left little doubt in her mind about who they were. "Two young men and a young woman?"

Norma looked surprised at first but quickly realized how Sadie knew them. "Are they guests of yours, dear?"

"Yes," she said. "And this is the second time I've heard someone complain about them."

"Well, hopefully they don't stay in town for very long. And if they *did* start the fire, I hope they get what's coming to them. They could have killed someone."

Sadie barely registered Norma's words, because her gaze had fixed on someone else who was standing near the back of the crowd, Bryan Parks. He was standing next to a pretty woman his own age with long, wavy brown hair, who was clutching his hand and whispering in his ear.

Not taking her eyes off him for even a second, Sadie walked away from the others without explanation, only vaguely aware of Sam following. She saw the moment Bryan recognized her because he ducked his head, said something to the woman, and then both of them slipped away from the crowd. They turned into an alley, and by the time Sadie reached it, they had vanished.

She might not have been able to talk to him, but she was certain of who she saw, which meant she now knew for a fact that Ivy's owner wasn't lying in a hospital somewhere.

He had abandoned her on purpose, and there was no excuse for that.

CHAPTER FIVE

Sadie and Sam waited with the others until the fire was out, and Bailey was sure she didn't need any help beyond what Hunter could provide. It sounded like the majority of the damage was smoke damage, other than a few scorched bricks, a section of the floor that would need to be replaced, and a warped door. Sadly, all of Bailey's current stock of cookies would have to be discarded, but the young woman just seemed grateful that the incident had ended in only minor losses.

Before she left, she told Sam about everything that had been going on since last night. He looked amused at the mention of the skunk ape, which hadn't come up when they were hanging out yesterday evening, but sobered quickly when she told him about the abandoned dog.

That's cruel, he signed. *And you saw him just now?*

"Yeah," she said. "Which tells me he has to have abandoned her on purpose. He's obviously still in town, and he hasn't come back to check on her once. It's been a full day by now; if we hadn't found her, she would have been without water for twenty-four hours."

I'm glad she's safe now, he signed. *Don't give her back unless he has a very good explanation.*

"Trust me, we aren't letting her go back to him until we get some answers. We've already involved the sheriff; that's why he was there earlier."

Sam promised to come over later that night to meet Ivy and hang out for a while. Sadie kissed him goodbye and waved as he crossed the road to where he had left his truck. He had to get back to work, and so did she.

When she turned her SUV on and saw the state of her gas tank, she realized she should stop for fuel before going back to the motel. She sent Penny a quick text before she left, letting her know that Bailey was fine, the damage was minimal, and that she would be back in about twenty minutes.

On the way back, she stopped at her usual gas station, which was a short detour out of town, just a couple miles away from the motel. It was the same gas station where Joshua, a young man who had unrequited feelings for Penny, worked. He was friendly enough, and she usually looked forward to chatting with him for a few minutes whenever she stopped for fuel, but when she went inside today, she was greeted by a stranger.

He was an older man who seemed to be having trouble ringing up the sodas Sadie had picked out herself and Penny. She watched as he muttered in frustration, squinting at the tiny numbers on the price tags.

"Can you tell what that's supposed to say?"

"That's a three," she said, glancing at the tag.

"Right. Sorry about that." He sighed. "My eyes aren't what they used to be. I haven't worked the register in years. If I ring this up wrong, you've got Joshua to thank for dropping the ball on us this morning.""

"What happened?" Sadie asked, immediately curious. "Did he get fired?"

The older man snorted. "No. He just didn't show up, and I can't get him on the phone. Don't know what happened. He's been a good, reliable employee for a long time now. Guess it just goes to show you can't count on the youth these days. If he shows his face around here again, I'm going to send him packing. I've got no use for an employee that isn't reliable."

Sadie personally thought Joshua should have earned a little more goodwill than that; he was almost always at the gas station and didn't seem to slack off much while he was working, but she wasn't about to tell someone else how to run their business. Maybe there had been other issues she wasn't aware of.

"Well, I'm sure he'll turn up," she said.

"You've got more faith than I do. Have a nice day, miss."

"You too."

Back at the motel, she found things pretty much how she had left them, with Penny and Ivy in the lobby, and the parking lot about half full. A lot of their guests had things to do during the day, but she knew it would be jam-packed again tonight.

She went upstairs to put Jasper and Angus on their leashes so she could take them outside for a potty break before she focused on work. When they reached the lobby, she observed Ivy as they went by. The Australian Shepherd seemed interested in the dogs, but not at all aggressive, which was a good sign.

"I'll need your help to introduce them later," Sadie told Penny. "I don't have time right now, though. How has she been behaving?"

"She's been an angel," Penny said. She had dragged the dog bed across the room so Ivy could lay behind the front desk. "I haven't seen any sign of her owner, though, and no one's called about her."

Sadie wrinkled her nose. "I saw him in town. Give me two seconds to take these guys out to do their business, then I'll tell you everything."

Sadie finished taking care of Jasper and Angus and then went into the back to check on the boarding dogs before she sat down with Penny to begin telling her about the fire at Sunshine Desserts and who she had seen there.

She had to start over when Cody came in and wanted to hear the details, but when she finished, both of them were furious.

"How could someone abandon this sweet girl?" Cody asked. He crouched, and Ivy rushed over to him, squirming gleefully into his arms as he pet her. "There's no doubt about it now, is there?"

"Yeah, that guy's a jerk," Penny said. "You said he looked fine?"

"Yep," Sadie said. "He was watching the commotion with some woman who I didn't recognize. He didn't look worried or hurt, but when he realized I had seen him, he got out of there pretty quickly, which tells me he knows what he did to Ivy is wrong."

"Well, what now?" Penny asked. "You said we don't have room for her, but I'm not sure if Sheriff Islington even registered what you said since he got the call about the fire right afterward. Should we take her to the animal shelter? They have a hold period for strays, right?"

Sadie shook her head, negating the idea immediately. "No way," she said. "We'll figure something out."

"You don't think you can put her upstairs with Jasper and Angus?" Cody asked.

"I mean, she seems like she's pretty easygoing," Sadie said. "But I'm not sure it's a good idea. I could gate her in the kitchen, but that's where I've been leaving Angus, since he still has that issue with trying to get at my shoes. And I don't want to leave her in a crate all day, that's not fair to her. If it was just for a few hours or even a day or two, it might be different, but we have no idea how long she'll here."

"Well, what if there was someone who could take Angus?"

Sadie sighed. "The sheriff *did* say I can legally

rehome him now, but I don't want to rush finding him a new home."

Cody looked horrified. "Wait, you're going to adopt him out? I thought we had more time."

"He's been here for months," Sadie said. She felt bad; Cody and Angus had developed a special bond. Cody often stayed after work to spend time with him, and Angus was a great dog for him to practice his training skills on. The two adored each other.

"*I* could take him home," Cody suggested. "I mean, just for a couple days while you have Ivy here. I can set up a big crate for him, if I can borrow one from here. I'll go home during lunch to walk him, so he isn't cooped up all day."

Sadie hesitated. Angus wasn't her dog, not really. Well, she was in charge of rehoming him, and the sheriff hadn't asked for any sort of input in the matter. Maybe he technically *was* her dog now that his previous owner's next of kin had decided they didn't want him. The more she thought about it, the more she couldn't see any reason to turn Cody down. He was an employee at the motel, and he had worked for them long enough that she knew he was a responsible person — especially when it came to the dogs — and he would take good care of Angus.

And Angus loved him. Both of them would be

happy with this solution, and it meant that she could keep Ivy behind the gate in her kitchen while they were trying to figure out what was going on with her owner.

"Well… all right," she said. "You can take him until Ivy's situation is resolved." Cody's face lit up, and she quickly added, "Just for a couple of days. And we are going to have to start looking for a new owner for him once all of this stuff with Ivy is straightened out, okay?"

"Yeah, sure," he said. "I'll bring him home with me this evening."

He checked the clock; his shift didn't end for another few hours, but she got the feeling he was going to be counting down the minutes.

With that figured out, she and Penny agreed to take turns watching Ivy in the lobby for the rest of the afternoon. Penny had a few things she wanted to do on the computer, and Cody had a few chores he still had to take care of in the kennel, so she left them to it while she went outside to check on the status of Room Four. Cody had done a great job cleaning the carpet and had left the door propped open so it could air out. The garbage that had been spread across the side yard had been cleaned up too.

Things were back to normal at the motel... sort of. Neil, Rory, and Kelsey weren't anywhere to be seen, and Sadie guessed they were exploring one of the many natural areas surrounding Greencreek in hopes of finding the skunk ape. She didn't expect them to have much success, but she hoped they were having fun and not causing trouble for anyone else. If they *did* start the fire at Sunshine Desserts, she hoped the sheriff found evidence to connect them to the crime before someone ended up seriously hurt.

While she was prepared to believe they had littered the garbage across the grass at the motel, the thought of them committing arson was a stretch. The garbage could be a ploy to draw attention to the skunk ape, or an attempt to prank someone, but what was the point of starting a fire in the middle of town? Maybe it was someone else entirely, but if Bailey had a suspect in mind, she wasn't telling.

Sadie was helping Cody load all of Angus's supplies into his car, along with a big crate she was letting him borrow, when Penny came out of the lobby with her phone pressed to her ear and waved her over urgently.

"It's Sheriff Islington," she called out. "He wants to talk to us both."

"I'll be right there," Sadie said.

She turned to Cody and Angus and crouched down to give the border collie a kiss on his furry head. "You be good, buddy. I'll see you in a couple days." Standing up, she turned to Cody. "Thanks for taking him. I'm sure you won't have any issues, but if you do, call me any time, day or night."

"Thanks for letting me bring him home," Cody said. He looked down and patted the dog, who gazed up at him adoringly. "We're going to have a great time. I'll see you Monday."

"Have a good weekend."

She waved as he got into his vehicle with Angus in the backseat, then turned to go into the lobby. Penny was waiting for her impatiently, and as soon as she shut the door behind her, she put the phone on speaker.

"All right, we're here," she said. "Did you find Ivy's owner?"

"No," Sheriff Islington's voice was tense and worried. "Sorry, but that isn't my priority right now. Something else happened, and I'm afraid it involves your motel. About half an hour ago, we got an emergency call from the state forest trailhead on West Creek Road about two miles outside of town. When I arrived, the good Samaritans led me to a body that had been burned past the point of recognition… and I discovered one of your room keys lying in the leaf litter just inches outside of the burn radius."

CHAPTER SIX

The first and most pressing question was which of their guests had been the victim of such a brutal crime, but that was a question no one had the answer to yet, not even Sheriff Islington. Her gut told her it was most likely to be one of the trio who was hunting the skunk ape – Neil, Rory, or Kelsey. She knew they were planning on exploring the state forest, and if they really were the ones who had lit the fire at Sunshine Desserts, then they would have had accelerant on hand.

"I'm going to send Deputy Francis by with the room key to see if you can match it to a guest," the sheriff said. "He'll be there in about fifteen minutes. In the meantime, keep your eyes peeled for anything unusual. We don't know what this is yet, and I want y'all to be careful."

"Was he..." Penny hesitated, clutching the phone so tightly her knuckles turned white. Ivy whined and leaned against her leg, sensing the heightened emotions in the room. "Was the victim alive when the fire was lit?"

"Thankfully, I don't believe so," the sheriff said. "It looks like cause of death was blunt force trauma to the head. Small mercies. It's not much, but it's something."

He ended the call shortly after that, leaving Sadie and Penny to wait in worried silence for the deputy to arrive.

It was a little more than fifteen minutes before he pulled into the parking lot. Sadie had met Deputy Francis before, but only briefly. His head was on a swivel as he entered the lobby, and he walked with none of the confidence Sheriff Islington had. She remembered the sheriff saying that he was new on the job — that was a couple of months ago, but it seemed that he still didn't have much experience. Greencreek was usually a quiet town, but she imagined a day like today would run even the most experienced law enforcement officers ragged.

"Are you the owners?" he asked, looking between

Sadie and Penny. His gaze dipped briefly toward Ivy, then back up to them.

"That's right," Penny said. She extended a hand. "Penelope Montgomery, but you can call me Penny."

Looking a little bemused, he shook her hand and turned to Sadie, who introduced herself as well.

"I heard you found one of our room keys at the crime scene," she said, once the basics were out of the way.

"Right." He reached into his pocket and withdrew a room key that was nestled inside a small, plastic evidence bag.

They didn't put the room numbers on the keys in an effort to keep a lost key from becoming an immediate security breach, but each of the keys was color-coded with a rubberized key cover that had the motel's name on the front. They changed the colors around every month as an added security measure, but Sadie usually had them memorized in the first few days.

She knew as soon as she saw the light blue key cover that the key belonged to Room Four. She exchanged a look with Penny. None of this made any sense — and it hadn't from the moment Bryan Parks abandoned his dog at the motel. She had seen him just hours ago. What had happened in that amount of time that led to his violent death?

"I'm supposed to get information about whoever was staying in this room," Deputy Francis prodded. "Do I need to request a warrant?"

"No," Penny said. She handed Sadie Ivy's leash and slipped behind the front desk to sit down in front of her computer. "I'll get the information for you. We already know who the guest was, though."

While Penny prepared to print out all of the information they had on Bryan, Sadie gave his name to Deputy Francis and explained the initial issue with Ivy being left alone in the room overnight. She wasn't sure if Sheriff Islington had a chance to tell Deputy Francis what was going on. Like he said, Ivy wasn't at the top of his list of priorities right now. She was safe with them, but whoever killed Bryan Parks was still out there, which meant other people might be in danger.

Their old printer was chugging away when Sadie heard a car door slam outside and loud voices chatting and laughing from the parking lot. She moved over to the lobby window to peer outside and saw Neil, Rory, and Kelsey piling out of their beat-up old SUV. It had a Bigfoot bumper sticker on the back and a decal of what she thought might be the Loch Ness Monster on the rear window.

"Let's get some cookies," she heard Neil say. "I'm hooked on those things."

"We're going to pay more for them if we get them here," Kelsey complained. "Why don't we just wait until tomorrow and see if that cookie shop is open again?"

"The sign on the window said it was closed for repairs, so there's no telling when it'll reopen," Neil said. "I don't care if I have to spend an extra couple bucks. We're on vacation. Live a little, Kelsey."

Kelsey rolled her eyes but followed Neil toward the lobby. Rory trailed behind, looking annoyed. Sadie stepped back from the window as they opened the lobby door. All three of them paused to give Deputy Francis wary looks. He looked right back at them, his eyes narrowing in suspicion.

"I see some familiar faces," he muttered. "You three are the ones who called the burn victim in, aren't you?"

Kelsey nodded, her jaw tight. "That was us. What are you doing here, sir? Are we in trouble?"

Deputy Francis raised an eyebrow. "Should you be in trouble?"

All three of them shook their heads. The deputy looked unconvinced. "Bit of a coincidence, isn't it? The victim was a guest at the motel you three are staying at, and you were the ones who found his body."

"He was a guest here?" Kelsey looked horrified.

Neil just snorted. "Look, dude, we were doing a good deed by telling the police we found the body. You're crazy if you think we killed him." He paused, then added with a grin, "I wonder if skunk apes can light fires."

"Dude, quit it," Rory said, nudging him with his elbow. "You shouldn't joke about stuff like that."

"No, I'm serious," Neil said. "It could help explain why they've managed to stay hidden for so long. They're smart. Maybe they've figured out how to make fire. Early humans could do it; why couldn't they?"

"I'll add 'skunk ape' to the top of our list of suspects," Deputy Francis said, his voice flat and unimpressed. "Do you have anything useful to add?"

"We weren't involved with this at all, sir," Kelsey said. "I know it's a big coincidence, but we were pretty deep in the woods for hours and we really didn't see or hear anything until we returned to the trailhead. I don't know what else to tell you."

"Are we free to go?" Rory asked.

Deputy Francis nodded. "You can head back to your rooms, but I hope you're not planning on leaving town anytime soon. We might need to ask you some more questions later."

The three fled the lobby, cookie-less and spooked by the presence of law enforcement. Sadie watched them go as Penny held up a freshly printed page of paper triumphantly and handed it over to Deputy Francis.

"Here's everything we have on Bryan Parks," she said.

"Thanks. Can I see the room he was in?"

Penny hesitated. "Well, sure, I can show it to you. But it was cleaned pretty thoroughly a couple hours ago. I'm afraid you won't find much."

Deputy Francis gave a put-upon sigh, pocketed the paper, and said, "Go on. I might as well take a look anyway."

CHAPTER SEVEN

After a quick investigation of Room Four, Deputy Francis left. It was almost time for Sadie to begin her daily walks with the boarding dogs, but first, she took a break to drink some coffee and sit in the lobby while Penny took Ivy on a short walk around the motel's lawn. She was glad Penny and the sweet Australian Shepherd had connected. Now that she thought about it, she could have asked Penny if Ivy could stay in her room, but maybe it was for the best that Ivy would be staying upstairs in her apartment. They already knew Ivy barked when left alone, and she was bound to disturb other guests if she was locked in Penny's room during the day.

After Penny and Ivy returned, Sadie began taking the boarding dogs on their long, enriching walks through the woods. When she finished almost two hours later, she left them all with ear scratches and treats, then went upstairs to get Jasper for his walk. It felt strange not taking Angus with her too — she had gotten used to having him around the past couple of months. Even though she knew getting him into a good home that had a job for him to do, whether that was herding or sports, would be the best thing for him, she felt a pang at the thought of rehoming him to a stranger. She would miss him this weekend, but at least she knew she would see him again soon, and she had no doubt that Cody would take great care of him.

She was just finishing up Jasper's walk — it turned out to be more of a jog, really, since he'd had a boring day and had a lot of excess energy — when she saw Sam pull into the parking lot in his old pickup truck. Another vehicle was close behind him. She didn't pay much attention to it as she jogged over to his truck with Jasper by her side and waved him forward to indicate that he should pull onto the grass. There weren't many parking spaces left, and she wanted to save them for the guests.

When the other vehicle followed him onto the grass and parked next to his truck, she glanced toward it, about to tell the guest that they could take one of the parking spaces, when she realized the driver was

Bailey. She was surprised; Bailey almost never came to the motel. Sadie suspected that like many locals, she had a bad feeling about the place given its reputation.

Sam got out of his truck and patted his thighs, and Sadie unhooked Jasper's leash to let the happy foxhound race over to him. She followed at a more sedate pace while Jasper wrestled with Sam. After a second, she whistled to him and patted her leg. Jasper trotted over to her and sat at her side, panting happily.

Hey, Sam signed to her.

"Hey, yourself," she said.

He pulled her into a hug. She leaned her head against his shoulder, relaxing into the comfort of his arms. It had been a crazy day, and she was glad she would get a few hours with him this evening.

Except it seemed like it wouldn't be time *alone* with him.

She pulled back and glanced at Bailey, who was still behind the wheel of her vehicle, doing something on her phone.

"What's up?" she asked. "I didn't know Bailey was planning on coming over too."

She kept her tone mild. She didn't want it to sound like Bailey wasn't welcome; of course she was. Bailey occupied a space somewhere between acquaintance and friend, and Sadie was always glad to spend more time with her. She just hadn't been expecting a visit tonight.

She caught me while I was leaving the hardware store, Sam signed. *She asked if I thought you'd mind if she dropped by the motel later tonight. I told her I was on my way there, and she was welcome to tag along. I hope that's all right.*

"Of course," she said. "I wonder what she wants?"

He shrugged, and they both turned toward Bailey's vehicle. This time she looked up at them, gave a brief wave, and unbuckled her seatbelt.

"Hey!" she called out as she rounded the front of her vehicle to join Sadie and Sam on the other side. She looked down at Jasper, who gazed up at her, his tail wagging. "We've met a few times, buddy. Do you remember me?"

She held out a hand for him to sniff, and when Sadie released him, he trotted over to greet her.

While she was occupied with the foxhound, Sam signed to Sadie, *I need to run home and take care of my dogs. Is the Australian Shepherd still here?*

"Yeah, she is. Cody took Angus home for the weekend, and Ivy is going to be staying in my apartment with me and Jasper until we figure out what's going on. I have a lot to tell you, but it can wait until you get back. We still have to do formal introductions between her and Jasper, but I'm sure they'll be fine. Jasper gets along with almost every dog he meets, and she seems like a sweetheart."

In that case, I won't bring Briar and Rose over tonight. They might be a bit much for her.

She felt bad to exclude the coonhounds, but she knew he was right. Poor Ivy had had a stressful day already, and she needed some time to wind down and get used to Jasper before bed.

"Take your time with them," she said, giving him a quick kiss on the cheek. "Penny and I were thinking about ordering pizza, and it usually takes about forty minutes to get here on a Friday night, so there's no rush. I'll see you soon."

He nodded and set off on foot for his house, pausing to wave at Bailey as he passed her. Bailey looked up from Jasper and waved back, then turned to smile at Sadie.

"Sorry to crash your evening," she said. "I was hoping to talk to you about something, and Penny too, if she's in."

"You're always welcome," Sadie said. "Let's head into the lobby. Our office hours ended a little while ago, so things *should* be pretty quiet for the rest of the evening, but on a day like today, who knows."

Penny was just as surprised to see Bailey as Sadie had been, but she greeted the other woman warmly. "I heard about the fire. I'm so glad no one got hurt…"

The three of them spent a couple of minutes catching up before Sadie asked Penny and Bailey to join her outside so they could walk Jasper and Ivy next to each other. They started the dogs a few feet apart but gradually moved them closer until the two dogs were able to sniff each other.

Ivy seemed a little wary of Jasper at first — the foxhound was larger than her and a lot more energetic — but when he dropped into a play bow, she reciprocated. When the two began to play as much as the confines of their leashes allowed, Sadie knew they would be just fine.

They locked the door when they returned to the lobby to make sure no one could accidentally let Ivy out, then Sadie unclipped the dogs' leashes to let them roam around the room and mingle while the three humans talked.

"I don't even know where to begin," Bailey said. She sat on one of the uncomfortable chairs in the waiting area and grimaced.

Penny pulled the rolling chair out from behind the

desk. "Here, you should sit in this one. I'm pretty sure those other chairs were meant to be torture devices."

"Thanks." Bailey moved over to the rolling chair and leaned back with a sigh. "That's better. Today has been one of the most stressful days of my life, and from what I've been hearing, I'm not the only one."

"I think it's been a tough day for the whole town," Sadie said. "I know it's been crazy here at the motel. You should go first, though. You said you wanted to talk about something?"

Bailey wrinkled her nose. "Yeah, this is probably going to sound weird, but do you two remember Calvin Deering? I think you knew Brian Deering, his uncle."

"Yeah, I remember him," Sadie said. "Hunter mentioned he has been stopping by the cookie shop a lot this week."

Bailey rolled her eyes. "Of course he did. Hunter couldn't keep his mouth shut if his life depended on it."

"What about him?" Sadie asked. "Do you need help? Is he bothering you?"

"Yes... Well, no." Bailey sighed. "Sort of. He asked me out Thursday evening, and I politely turned him down. Mostly because I'm honestly not looking to date right now. I'm way too focused on Sunshine

Desserts. The business has been growing rapidly, and I've even been thinking of hiring another employee; I just don't have time for much of a personal life. I'm sure you know how that is."

Sadie let out a quiet huff of laughter. "Yeah, we do."

"I don't even remember the last time I had a full day off," Penny added. "That's a major reason I haven't been dating either. I don't know how Sadie manages it."

"Well, it's a little easier to date someone when they live right next door and have a flexible schedule," Sadie said. "Anyway, Bailey, how did Calvin take it when you turned him down?"

"That's the thing," Bailey said. "He seemed fine — I told him I was happy to keep getting to know him as a friend. but I was too focused on work to think about anything else right now. And he acted like he understood, but… then the fire happened. I can't help but wonder if he might have been involved. No one I know knows him very well. From what I've gathered, he left town for a while after his uncle passed away but then came back and moved into his uncle's old house and he's mostly been keeping to himself. since then. You two are somehow always involved in everything," she added. "So, I was wondering if you'd heard anything about him. Do you think he's the sort of person who would try to get revenge after someone turned him down?"

Penny shrugged, and Sadie said, "I have no idea. It might be worth looking into, but if he didn't do it, he'll probably be offended if he finds out you think he did."

"That's what I'm worried about," Bailey said. "He seems nice enough – maybe a bit lonely and a little too serious — and I don't want to make him feel uncomfortable right after he moved to town by sending the sheriff to question him. The fire really scared me, though. I don't know why anyone would do something like that. I sell cookies, for goodness' sake; it's not like it's a controversial business."

"Do you think Norma might have been right, when she said it was those three people from out of town?" Sadie asked. "The ones who are obsessed with the skunk ape; they're staying here, just so you know."

It was Bailey's turn to shrug. "Maybe? They came into my store a couple hours before the fire. I can see why Norma thought they were being a little obnoxious, but they seemed friendly and happy to be here. They were polite when I rang them up, and they seemed to really like the cookies. I have no idea why they would come back later just to light my store on fire."

She groaned and leaned back in her seat again. "I'm not going to be able to sleep a wink until I know who did this. What if whoever it was comes back and burns my store down overnight? And business has been doing so well lately, too. We've been getting more regular deliveries to businesses in the area, and now that the Forgotten Retreat is up and running again, I'm hoping we'll have even more customers soon. How am I supposed to keep up with the demand if I'm afraid to be in Sunshine Desserts alone?"

"Could you hire security?" Penny asked. "Just temporarily, until all of this gets solved. Or maybe install some security cameras in the alley behind the building?"

"You know, I probably *could* hire someone to keep an eye on the place," Bailey said. "I don't know about security cameras. I have one inside, looking over the register, but the back of the building is all brick and cinder block, and my Wi-Fi signal doesn't pass through it very well, so I'd have to install a wired security system. I lease the storefront, which means I'd have to get written permission from the owner, and I'd have to get someone to drill through the brick for me…" She trailed off and shook her head. "I think I'll look into security first. It'll probably be expensive but just having someone to keep an eye on the place, maybe drive by a few times a night, and someone I can call if I get spooked while I'm there alone would help a lot. Thanks, you two. I think I just needed someone to talk to, someone who understands what I'm going through. I know you've been through a lot here at the motel, and it makes me feel better knowing I'm not going through this alone."

"Anytime," Sadie said. "I mean it, you're always welcome here."

"And I'm sure all this will be resolved soon," Penny added. "Arson is one of those crimes that gets taken pretty seriously."

"Especially now that someone died," Sadie said.

"What do you mean?" Bailey asked. "Someone died?"

Sadie realized the news might not have spread yet. Bryan Parks had only been murdered a few hours ago, and as far as she knew, the only people outside of law enforcement who had seen his body were the three out-of-towners.

Sadie almost wished she hadn't brought it up, because she knew that what she was about to say would only make Bailey more frightened, but she thought it was important the other woman knew.

There was a chance that the same person was behind both fires, and if they were willing to kill, then Bailey deserved to be warned.

Taking a deep breath, she told Bailey about the murder of Bryan Parks. The other woman listened raptly, her expression slowly growing more horrified.

"You probably shouldn't spread this last part around," she added when she was done, "but the people who found him were the same people Norma was complaining about. The three out-of-towners who are looking for the skunk ape."

"No way," Bailey breathed. "That's some coincidence, isn't it? If it was them, *why*? The guy who died was a guest at your motel too, right?"

Sadie nodded. That was a connection she hadn't made yet, but it could explain a possible motive for them, if the trio had somehow run afoul of Bryan while he was here. That might be a little more likely if he had actually *been* at the motel for any significant amount of time.

There was too much going on, and it was giving her a headache. If only she could find that woman who had been with Bryan while everyone was watching the firefighters handle the fire at Sunshine Desserts. If anyone had answers, it was her.

A thought struck her like a lightning bolt. "Loretta

has two guests, right?" Sadie asked. "Hunter said they were a couple on their honeymoon."

"Yeah, she was bragging about them when she came in to pick up some cookies," Bailey said. "They arrived on Thursday, and I guess they're planning on staying until early this coming week. She seems to think they're heralding the revival of her bed and breakfast."

"Did she tell you anything else about them? Descriptions or names?"

Bailey shook her head. "No. Why?"

"It doesn't matter. It's probably nothing."

Despite her words, her mind was racing. Bryan had to have been staying somewhere, and he definitely wasn't staying at the motel. The bed and breakfast was the only other place in town that offered overnight rooms. Was *that* where he and the mystery woman had been staying? And if so, was the woman still there?

CHAPTER EIGHT

Bailey stayed just long enough to share a couple slices of pizza with them and sample one of her own cookies from the motel's stock before leaving. Penny went to bed early, in order to give Sadie some alone time with Sam. They spent the rest of the evening up in her apartment, talking about the recent spate of crimes around town and watching Ivy explore her new temporary home.

Before she went to bed, Sadie set up a cozy space in the kitchen for Ivy with water and food bowls, one of Jasper's extra dog beds, and a few of the toys that Ivy seemed to favor. She wanted the dog to get used to the space overnight, so if there were any issues, she would be there to address them. Come tomorrow, Sadie would be leaving the dogs up here while she went downstairs to work. At least Jasper's presence meant Ivy wouldn't be completely alone; they could keep each other company through the gate.

She didn't hear a peep out of Ivy all night, but she still tossed and turned. Something bad was going on in town, and she wanted to get to the bottom of it… especially since three of the main suspects were staying right here at the motel. By the time morning came, she had the beginnings of a plan, though it was a sketchy one and relied on her hunch from the night before being correct.

During her lunch break, she would drive to Loretta's bed and breakfast and try to speak with her guests — or rather, her one remaining guest. If Sadie was right, then Bryan's wife would be there alone, and likely grieving her husband's passing.

If that was the case, Sadie didn't want to bother her too much, but she needed to know if the woman knew anything about what was going on – and in return, maybe she could give the woman some answers herself. She had to be just as hungry for the truth as Sadie was.

The morning seemed to creep past, almost as if fate itself was against her. No sooner had she finished cleaning the kennels than one of the dogs made a mess inside, so she had to get the disinfectant and all the cleaning supplies out all over again. Then someone stopped by to try to drop off a golden retriever. They swore up and down that they had a reservation for this weekend, but neither Sadie nor Penny could find it on the schedule — and even if they had accidentally double-booked someone, they simply didn't have the space to take another dog.

Finally, the person realized they had the wrong place entirely and were supposed to go forty minutes further down the road to a vet clinic that did small-scale boarding. Sadie did her best to be understanding of the mistake, but after spending half an hour nearly pulling her hair out because she was worried they had ruined someone's vacation, it was hard not to scream her frustration.

Finally, noon rolled around. Sadie was eager to get going, but she let Penny take her lunch break first. She wasn't sure how long this was going to take and didn't want to have to worry about holding her friend up while she was talking to Bryan's wife... if she was even right about where the couple had been staying.

Finally, *finally,* Penny returned from her lunch break with an iced coffee in hand, and Sadie was free to snatch up her purse and hurry out to the parking lot. Despite being fully booked, many of their guests were out and about enjoying the nice weather, so she had plenty of space to back out of her spot and pull onto the road. She decided to take the back roads into town; Greencreek's downtown area was bound to be busy at lunchtime on a Saturday, and the bed and breakfast was clear on the other side of town anyway. The back roads would lead her right to the quiet neighborhood on the outskirts of town where the building was located.

She turned left onto Highway 78 and, a mile down the road, turned right at the stop sign onto the road that led her past the gas station. She glanced at it as she drove by but was going too fast to see through the window. She wondered if Joshua had ever come back, and if so, if he had been fired. She hoped she would run into him again at some point, if only to get the full story.

She turned onto one of the quiet, wooded rural roads that would eventually lead her into town, only for another car to pull out of a driveway right ahead of her. She slowed down, grumbling, but was glad when the car quickly got up to full speed.

Her relief turned to horror a moment later, when something brown and furry ran out of the undergrowth on one side of the road and attempted to cross in front of the car. The car couldn't brake in time and ended up clipping the creature, sending it spinning into the ditch on the other side of the road. For a second, the car's brake lights flared, but then it sped up again, apparently deciding it wasn't worth stopping.

Sadie, who had only gotten a glimpse of the creature and had no idea what it might be — oddly, it looked like it was walking upright — slowed and pulled over onto the shoulder of the road. She glanced in her side mirror at the ditch where the thing had disappeared but didn't see any signs of movement.

She was torn between getting out and checking on the animal, and the pragmatic worry that an injured animal of that size might be dangerous. Especially if it was a bear, which seemed the closest match to the large, shaggy, bipedal form she had seen.

Regardless of what the creature was, she couldn't just leave it lying there, injured and possibly dying. In the end, she took her cell phone and her pepper spray with her and left the SUV running with the driver's door open in case she needed to make a quick escape.

She crossed the road cautiously, with the pepper spray held out in front of her in case the creature charged at her. As she got closer to the ditch, she heard a groan that didn't sound like any animal she recognized. Creeping the last few steps forward, she peered into the ditch and saw a hairy, ape-like face looking up at her.

Sadie shrieked and jumped back. She almost depressed the button on the pepper spray when a weak voice called out, "Wait, I'm in a costume!"

Sadie blinked and lowered the pepper spray, inching forward until she was peering into the ditch again. The creature's furry paw raised to pull at the shaggy coat on top of its head. When it did, the creature's entire face began to move – it was a mask. When it was off, Kelsey squinted up at her.

"You're that woman from the motel, aren't you?" She tried to get up but fell back with a groan.

"Oh, my goodness." Sadie shoved her phone and the pepper spray into her pockets, then crouched and reached out toward the injured woman. She hesitated at the last second, worried that trying to help her get up might worsen her injuries. "Are you okay? And yeah, I'm Sadie, from Sit, Stay, Sleep Motel and Boarding."

"I don't think anything is broken," Kelsey said. On her second attempt, she managed to sit up and reached down to feel at her left hip.

"Hold on, I'll call 911," Sadie said, reaching for the pocket her phone was in.

Kelsey shook her head. "I don't need an ambulance. They barely clipped me. Getting thrown into the ditch is what hurt the most."

"Are you sure? Even if you don't need an ambulance, that person just committed a hit and run."

Kelsey gave a dry laugh. "I'd rather they go on thinking they hit some sort of animal instead of finding out they hit a person. It was my own fault for being stupid and running out in front of them. I thought I had time to make it across the road. It's not their fault I jumped out in front of their car like that. Hold on, I'm going to try to stand."

Sadie rose to her feet so she would be ready to help Kelsey if she needed it, but Kelsey managed to stand up on her own. She swayed for a second, then began to strip the Bigfoot costume off, feeling at her injuries through the clothes she wore underneath.

"I don't think I'm bleeding much, just a few scratches from my tumble into the ditch." She twisted her body and moved her leg, then stepped forward, both legs taking her weight easily. "Yeah, nothing's broken, I've just got some bruises and bumps, that's all."

"Do you want me to drive you to the hospital so they can check you over?"

Kelsey shook her head again. "No way. I'm still on my parents' health insurance, and they'll have questions when the bill comes in. I really think I'm fine. Though, if you don't mind, could you give me a ride back to the motel?"

"Of course," Sadie said. "Do you need me to get someone to help bring your car back? Where did you park, anyway?"

Kelsey began to limp across the road. "Oh, I carpooled with the guys. They're out walking around in the forest somewhere. When they text to ask where I am, I'll just tell them I fell down a hill, and a good Samaritan helped me out."

She looked down at the costume, which was draped over her arm, then muttered, "Shoot, I forgot the head."

Before she could turn back to get it, Sadie said, "You can get in the car, I'll go back for it."

She jogged across the road and fetched the mask out of the ditch. Twigs and leaves were stuck in the fur, but it seemed undamaged. She remembered Norma saying something about one of the trio having a Bigfoot mask and frightening Mulberry when they put it on – this must have been it.

Kelsey was buckled into the passenger seat by the time she returned to the SUV. Sadie handed her the mask, got into the driver's seat, and hit her blinker to signal that she was going to turn around. After making sure the road was clear, she pulled away from the shoulder. Only once they were safely on their way back to the motel did she give in to her curiosity.

"Is this what you guys do, then? You fake Bigfoot sightings? Or skunk ape sightings, I guess."

"No, not usually," Kelsey said. "Neil's parents got him this costume as a graduation gift. He's been obsessed with Bigfoot and the skunk ape and every other cryptid for as long as I've known him, and he wears the costume every Halloween. He doesn't do fake sightings, though; he really believes Bigfoot, or whatever you want to call it, is real. I'm the one who suggested we bring it on the trip. I said if we do find a community of skunk apes, we might be able to get closer to them if someone's wearing the costume." She sighed. "What he and Rory didn't know is that I was planning to spice things up a little. I've been sneaking away to leave tracks in the mud, and today I woke up early and hid the costume in the back of the vehicle before the guys woke up. After we had been out there for a while, I pretended to get a call from my mom and said I needed to try to find an area with better service. I snuck back to the vehicle and put the costume on. I was planning on running past them while they were hiking – I know it would make Neil's year if he thought he saw a real skunk ape. I figured it wouldn't hurt to let some of the locals see me too, but as you can tell, that didn't exactly go to plan."

"Are you the one who spread the garbage across the grass at the motel?" Sadie asked.

Kelsey looked confused. "What? No. I wouldn't do something like that. I'm not about to vandalize someone else's property just to feed into Neil's fantasy. It was supposed to be harmless fun."

Sadie was both relieved and disappointed at Kelsey's answer. She seemed earnest, but for a second, Sadie thought she might have caught the suspect red-handed. If Kelsey was telling the truth, then she wasn't behind any of the crimes that had been happening around town.

If she wasn't, then who was?

CHAPTER NINE

She dropped Kelsey off at the motel, then turned around and headed back toward town. This time, she made it to the bed and breakfast uninterrupted. There were three cars in the gravel lot behind the building; she recognized Loretta's ancient sedan, and there were unfamiliar vehicles parked next to it.

She felt a surge of irritation at herself for not double-checking what vehicle Bryan drove. She and Penny had checked the security footage a couple days ago, but all she really remembered was that it was silver. Her eyes narrowed at the silver convertible. She wasn't completely sure, but she had a feeling that was it.

She took a second to check her appearance in the mirror before she went in. Satisfied that she didn't look like someone who had just had an encounter with Bigfoot, she grabbed her purse and marched up to the old house.

A little bell rang as she let herself inside. A moment later, from deeper in the building, she heard the low creak of another door opening. Shuffling footsteps preceded Loretta Browning as she came down the hall.

Her eyes narrowed when she saw Sadie. "Well, well, well," she said. "Are you scoping out the competition?"

"No." She glanced around the entranceway. Loretta had definitely cleaned the place up a little, but it was still cluttered, dusty, and looked run down. Privately, she didn't think the bed and breakfast was much in the way of competition, but it didn't matter. That wasn't why she was here. "I'm looking for…" She hesitated. She didn't know the mysterious woman's name, so she settled for, "Bryan Parks's wife."

Loretta frowned. "Well, we have a Parks staying here, but—"

"Thanks, Loretta. I can take it from here," another voice chimed in.

Sadie turned to see the mystery woman standing in the entrance to the common area. She gave Sadie a tight smile. "I'm Chelsea Parks. Do you mind if I ask why you're here?"

"Maybe it would be better if we sat down first," Sadie suggested..

Chelsea shrugged and stepped aside to gesture into the common area. "Sure, if that's what you want."

"I'll go make some tea," Loretta said.

She shuffled away, and Sadie walked into the common area to take a seat on one of the plush armchairs. Despite their age, they were quite comfortable.

Chelsea sat on the end of the couch closest to her. "I'm afraid I didn't catch your name."

"I'm Sadie Barton," Sadie explained. "I'm from Sit, Stay, Sleep Motel and Boarding, the motel on Highway 78 just outside of town."

"And why are you looking for Bryan?"

"It was actually you I wanted to talk to," Sadie said. "First, I just want to say I'm so sorry for your loss. I can't even imagine what you're going through, and while you were on your honeymoon, of all things."

Chelsea gave her a blank look. "I'm afraid you've lost me. First, we aren't on our honeymoon. Whoever told you that has the wrong information. The truth is, we came here as a last-ditch attempt to repair our relationship." She licked her lips and seemed to warm up to her story as she went on. "Bryan's been acting so strangely lately. He keeps disappearing at odd hours for no reason, he's constantly forgetting our poor dog in odd places, and he's even come close to being violent with me a few times."

"Is your dog an Australian Shepherd?" Sadie asked. Of course, if Chelsea was Bryan's wife, then Ivy was her dog too, but Sadie didn't want to give too much away too soon. This whole situation was strange.

Chelsea smiled. "Yes, a sweet little girl named Ivy. How do you know about her?"

She didn't know Ivy had been abandoned, Sadie realized. She took a deep breath. "On Thursday afternoon, your husband abandoned Ivy at our motel. He rented a room through Sunday, but all he did was drop the dog off and leave. He hasn't come back to check on her since. It's lucky we found her in time. Don't worry, she's safe and sound now."

Chelsea gasped and pressed a hand to her chest. "I had no idea. He said he dropped her off at the kennel, but I didn't know which one. What was he thinking? She could have died."

"That's what I was wondering," Sadie said. "I'm

wondering if he was having some sort of mental crisis leading up to his death. From what you said, it sounds like it's possible."

"I'm sorry, his death?" Chelsea looked surprised. It was possibly the most genuine emotion she had shown since Sadie got there. "My husband isn't dead. At least, not as far as I know."

Had the sheriff neglected to tell her about what happened? She couldn't imagine why he would have waited this long to notify Bryan's next of kin.

"He was found yesterday on a trailhead just outside of town?"

It came out as more of a question. Their wires had gotten crossed, and she didn't know how.

"Oh. That body wasn't my husband's," Chelsea said. "I think…" She faltered and took a deep breath before she started again. "I think Bryan might have killed someone. I haven't seen him since."

The body wasn't Bryan's? That was news to Sadie – but then again, Sheriff Islington didn't have any obligation to keep her and Penny up to date on the case. It made sense that Bryan's wife would have the most current information.

"If it wasn't Bryan, then who was it?" she asked.

"I have no idea," Chelsea said. "Some local, probably. When I spoke to law enforcement, they said they were going to look into missing people, but since it happened so recently, whoever it was might not have been reported missing yet."

Sadie wracked her mind. She had spoken to everyone she was closest to recently, and if someone who was a prominent figure in town, like Norma, was missing, she was sure she would have heard about it. The fact that the body didn't belong to any of her closest friends was a relief, but a minor one. If it really wasn't Bryan, then who could it be?

Joshua.

Her stomach sank at the thought. She didn't know if the young man was still missing; it was possible he had simply forgotten he was scheduled at the gas station the other day and he was perfectly fine other than possibly being out of a job, but she wouldn't be able to rest until she knew for sure.

"Why would Bryan do something like that?"

"I don't know," Chelsea replied. "Like I said, he hasn't been himself lately. I know my wedding vows were for better or for worse, but if he really did this, then I think it's the last straw. I can't be married to a man who would murder someone. Thank goodness Georgia offers at-fault divorce. Otherwise, I might be at risk of losing everything." She gave Sadie a wry smile. "The law really isn't set up for when the wife is the higher earner. There's no way I'm paying alimony to a man who's lost his marbles."

Sadie was at a loss. She had more questions than ever, but Chelsea didn't seem to know much more than she did. She glanced at the antique clock in the corner. She had already taken too long – she needed to get back to the motel.

She rose to her feet, unsatisfied about the way the conversation was ending. "I need to get going," she said, "but thanks for talking with me. Would you like to get Ivy now, or do you want to wait until things are a little more settled?"

"I'd like to at least see her and make sure she's okay," Chelsea said. "Give me a few minutes. I'm going to speak to Loretta and see if she's okay with me having a dog here, then I'll head to your motel. If Loretta allows it, I'll take Ivy with me tonight."

CHAPTER TEN

When she was half a mile away from the motel, Sadie got a text message from Penny that read, *Urgent!!! Where are you? Need you here NOW.*

She didn't bother replying since she was less than a minute out, but she did increase her speed a little. She turned into the parking lot and claimed the closest spot before grabbing her purse and jumping out of the vehicle to head straight for the lobby.

When she opened the lobby door, she saw a middle-aged blond man with blue eyes sitting in the waiting area. Penny was standing behind the desk, her arms crossed in front of her.

"There you are," she said. "I need you to help me figure this out."

"What's going on?" Sadie asked.

Instead of answering, Penny glanced at the man, who stood up and cleared his throat. He was on the shorter side; standing up, he was slightly shorter than Sadie herself.

"My name is Bryan Parks," he said, "and I believe you have my dog here somewhere. Her name is Ivy. She's a three year old tricolor Australian Shepherd."

"Do you have your ID on you?" Sadie asked, trying not to let her surprise and suspicion show. No wonder Penny's text message had sounded so freaked out.

She knew for a fact this was *not* the man who dropped Ivy off. That man had been tall with dark hair and glasses. She might not have been able to pick him out of a lineup of similar-looking people, but she could definitely tell him apart from the man who stood in front of her.

He reached into his pocket and took out his wallet, presenting her with his driver's license. The photo on it was a match, and sure enough, the name on it was Bryan Parks. She handed it to Penny.

"Can you see if the driver's license number on that is the same as the one we recorded when the Room Four guest checked in?"

Penny nodded and sat down in front of her computer to pull the information up.

"Look, I don't know what's going on, but can you just tell me whether you have my dog? Is she safe? Is she hurt?"

"It's a match," Penny said from behind the front desk. "The driver's license numbers are the same."

Sadie narrowed her eyes. The man who abandoned Ivy only had a temporary driver's license with him, which meant there hadn't been a picture on it. The temporary license must have been a fake; she imagined they were significantly easier to forge than a real ID card, and it wasn't as if she had looked up examples online to make sure it was legitimate. That told her that the man standing in front of her was almost certainly the real Bryan Parks.

The worry in his voice was genuine, and Sadie decided to answer his questions. She wouldn't tell him exactly where Ivy was just yet, but if he really was Ivy's owner, then she knew the sickening worry he must be experiencing right now.

"We have Ivy. She's fine," she said. "She was alone in one of our motel rooms for about eighteen hours, but as soon as we realized what was going on, we got her out of there, and we've been taking great care of her ever since. The motel doubles as a dog boarding and training kennel, so we have plenty of supplies on hand to make her comfortable. She has water, toys, a nice soft dog bed, and I fed her some of my own dog's good quality kibble. She's been a sweetheart the entire time."

"Thank goodness." Bryan looked so relieved that for a moment, Sadie was worried he was about to faint. "Can someone please tell me what's going on? She's been missing since Thursday, and when I checked my bank account this morning, I saw a fraudulent charge from this motel. I spent the last two days frantically looking for her, but it was like she vanished off the face of the Earth. The moment I saw the charge; I drove straight down here in case whoever had stolen my information had also stolen my dog. Can you tell me who dropped her off?"

"I don't know who dropped off," Sadie said. "He said his name is Bryan Parks. The room was paid for in advance, and he showed us what must have been a fake ID when he checked in."

"I think we should call the police," Penny said. "At the very least, this is a case of identity theft on top of the animal cruelty for abandoning Ivy, and it sounds like it might be dognapping too."

"Please do," Bryan said. "I want to get to the bottom of this. Now, can I please see my dog?"

Sadie hesitated, and before she could decide whether to bring Ivy down or not, she heard a car door slam outside. She opened the lobby door, wanting to see whether the new arrival needed something before she focused all of her attention on the question of Bryan and Ivy, only to realize the newcomer was Chelsea Parks. She had almost completely forgotten the woman was going to come check on Ivy.

Chelsea paused on the sidewalk right outside of the lobby, her eyes fixed on the man inside. Shock twisted her features. When he spoke, Bryan sounded just as surprised.

"Chelsea, what are you doing here?"

"I…" She trailed off, at a loss for words, and took a step backwards. "I have to go."

She turned and raced back to her car. Sadie saw her get into the passenger seat and realized someone else was in the driver's seat. The car backed out of its spot so quickly that the tires squealed on the asphalt. Bryan raced past Sadie and got into his own car. He cranked the engine and tore out of the parking lot after them.

Sadie shot a glance over her shoulder at Penny.

She already had her cell phone pressed to her ear and mouthed *police* at Sadie. Sadie nodded and ran outside to her SUV. She didn't want to get involved in a high-speed car chase, but someone needed to follow them and make sure no one got hurt.

CHAPTER ELEVEN

They didn't make it very far. No sooner had Sadie pulled out onto the road than Chelsea's car braked suddenly. Bryan's vehicle pulled up alongside it, but it was a trap. Chelsea's car swerved suddenly, smashing into Bryan's car and sending it skidding into the ditch. It didn't end there; whoever was driving Chelsea's car lost control and slid off the road too, pinning the passenger side door against a tree. Sadie felt a sense of déjà vu as she pulled over onto the shoulder, but this time Bigfoot wasn't to blame for the accident she had witnessed.

She got out of her SUV but hung back when she saw Bryan kick the door open and get out of his car. He looked shaken and was wiping at a bloody nose but wasted no time in running across the road to his wife's vehicle. He reached for the driver's side door, then recoiled as a man got out — a very familiar man, who was tall with dark hair and thick-rimmed, rectangular glasses.

He was the man who had been impersonating Bryan Parks.

Chelsea climbed across the seat, swearing up a storm. The man reached out to help her out of the vehicle. She scowled at the damage to her car but fell silent when Bryan called out her name.

"Who is this?" he asked his wife, his hands clenched into fists at his side. "What are you doing with him? I thought you were visiting your mom."

"Bryan, you're scaring me," Chelsea said.

"Are you the ones who took Ivy?" he continued. "Do you have any idea what I've been going through? I've been calling you all weekend, and you acted like you had no idea where she was."

"Stop, please," she pleaded. "Before someone gets hurt."

"What are you talking about? I'm not going to hurt anyone. I've never raised a hand to you in my life. I just want to know what's going on. Are you having an affair?"

Chelsea grabbed the taller man's arm. His jaw was clenched, and he was looking at Bryan like he wanted to hit him. "Brandon's just a friend," she explained. "I invited him along for my own safety. You haven't been in your right mind lately, Bryan, and I was worried about what would happen if I ran into you."

"*I* haven't been in my right mind?" Bryan said. "You lied to me about where you were going this weekend, and you stole my dog and abandoned her at a motel. *You're* the one who's not in your right mind!"

Chelsea clutched Brandon's arm tighter. "Bryan, I never said I was going to visit my mom, and you're the one who dropped Ivy off at the motel. I checked our bank statement. You used your card to reserve the room, and I'm certain the motel would have made you show ID when you checked in."

Bryan gaped at her. "I never did any of that. You know how much I love Ivy. I would never abandon her. And my card information was *stolen*... unless you're the one who made the reservation before you left."

"He's telling the truth," Sadie finally chimed in. "Bryan isn't the one who abandoned Ivy at the motel. *He* is." She nodded at Brandon, if that was really his name, who scowled at her.

"I've never seen you before in my life, woman, and I've definitely never been to your motel."

Sadie put her hands on her hips, though she stayed

near her SUV, well aware that the situation could devolve into violence in an instant. "Nice try, but we have security cameras, and we already shared the footage with law enforcement. The cameras caught you red-handed."

Chelsea's expression turned livid and she let go of Brandon's arm to begin smacking him. "I told you they have security cameras, you idiot! What happened to your disguise? You weren't supposed to show your face."

"Stop hitting me." Brandon pushed her away. "I didn't think it mattered, all right? I was just dropping off the dumb dog. I didn't think anyone would check the cameras. Plus, at places like that, the security cameras are usually fake."

"So, you're admitting it," Bryan said. "One of you, or both of you, stole Ivy and abandoned her at a motel. How could you do that, Chelsea? What if they hadn't found her until three or four days later? She could have *died*."

"You know what? I'm out," Brandon said before Chelsea could respond. "This has gone too far. If you want to blame someone, blame your wife. This whole thing was her idea. I told her she should man up and serve you the divorce papers, but she didn't want to be stuck paying you alimony for the rest of her life."

"I don't understand," Bryan said. "Divorce? What's going on?"

"Baby, you're imagining things," Chelsea said, taking a step toward him. "I think you need to see a doctor."

"Chelsea, it's over," Brandon snapped. He pushed his glasses further up his nose, then crossed his arms and turned his attention to Bryan. "She's been trying to make it look like you were having a psychotic break, but it's gone too far. It was her idea to drop your dog off at the motel. I helped her with that and with spreading some garbage on the grass, and I'm the one who left your phone there to pin it on you. We were trying to make it look like you had a complete mental break. I thought that would be enough, but she didn't want to stop there. I should have put an end to it when she lit that building on fire. She tried to spell your name with the accelerant, but I don't think it worked well because as far as I know, the police never linked it to you. She also spray-painted your initials all over one of the walls in that same alley. Honestly, man, this woman hates you." He turned to look at Chelsea. "And for the record, we're over. You're the craziest women I've ever had the misfortune of dating."

Chelsea gasped. "You can't leave me, Brandon. I turned my entire life on its head for you."

"And what happens when the next guy catches your attention?" Brandon asked. "I don't want to end up like this sad sack, with my crazy girlfriend trying to ruin my life."

"Hold on," Sadie said. She was still caught on the crimes Brandon had listed. One thing was missing. "Did you kill someone so you could pin it on your husband?"

Bryan blanched and looked at his wife in horror. Even Brandon looked shocked.

"What is she talking about?" he asked.

"I have no idea," Chelsea said. "She's making things up."

"There was a murder," Sadie said. "Yesterday. A man was found deceased in the state forest, and his body was burned.. They found the key to Room Four next to him."

Brandon looked sick. "I had no idea. You have to believe me. I wasn't involved in that."

"What's wrong with you?" Bryan whispered to his wife. "You *killed someone*? How could you do that?"

"It wasn't hard," Chelsea said. She finally seemed to drop the mask, and now her expression was cold and emotionless. "It was some guy I met at the gas station. I asked if he knew any good hiking places around here, and he said yes. Then I asked if he could show me, and he agreed to meet me there. Once we were in the woods and out of sight, I hit him over the head with a hammer I found at the bed and breakfast. I tucked it into my purse when I left to meet him and wiped it down before replacing it when I got back. Once I was sure he was dead, I lit his body on fire and left. I thought that would be what sealed it for you; them finding a room key registered to *your name* right next to a murdered man. That alone would put you away for at least thirty years, even if the rest of it wasn't enough to grant me the terms I wanted in the divorce."

Bryan stared at her. "I didn't mean the logistics, Chelsea. I meant how could you bring yourself to do something like that? I knew we've been having a rough patch, but that doesn't explain any of this."

"You're like a limpet, dragging me down and holding me back," Chelsea said. "When I found a *real* man, I knew I owed it to myself to do whatever it took to restart my life without you weighing me down anymore."

She reached for Brandon again, but he shook her off and backed away, glancing first at Bryan and then at Sadie. "I didn't know. I swear."

Chelsea opened her mouth to respond but then paused and tilted her head. "Do you hear that?"

A second later, Sadie did; sirens. The sheriff must be responding to Penny's call.

Chelsea's eyes widened and her voice grew panicked. "Someone called the police? How could you betray me like that? I'm not going to prison!"

She raced back to her car and tried to start the engine, but it sputtered and died. Brandon walked over and shut the door, then leaned against it so she couldn't get it open.

"You're not going anywhere," he said to her through the closed window. "You went too far, Chelsea. This is the end of the line for you. You deserve whatever sentence the judge hands down, and you had better believe I'm not going to let you drag me down with you."

EPILOGUE

The moment Ivy saw Bryan when Sadie brought her down to the lobby was the brightest part of Sadie's weekend. The Australian Shepherd turned into a bouncing ball of energy and joy as soon as she realized her owner was there. She raced around the lobby, slipping and sliding across the floor until she collided with Bryan's legs and flopped over onto her back, wagging her tail frantically. He sat down on the floor next to her and scratched her belly while murmuring about how much he had missed her and how glad he was that she was safe.

"Thank you," he said at last, looking up at Sadie and Penny. "Thank you so much for taking care of her. What do I owe you?"

"Nothing," Sadie said, "and we'll refund you for the motel room too."

"No, really, I should pay you something for everything you did."

"We're just glad we were able to reunite the two of you," Sadie said.

Technically, the whole mix-up was partially their fault; she should have been stricter about requiring a photo ID. If she had, some of this might have been avoided. On the other hand, if they hadn't let Brandon check into Room Four, there was no telling what he might have done with Ivy. Brandon might falter at the thought of murder, but he clearly didn't care about the dog in the slightest, and neither did Chelsea.

"Well, thank you so much," Bryan said. "Ivy's my world, especially now that I'm going to be going through a divorce and a long court case."

Sadie had no idea how one woman could cause so much chaos. Well, Brandon had helped with some of it, but it was clear Chelsea had been the driving force. She hadn't *just* wanted to divorce Bryan; she had wanted to completely destroy him. It was a level of intentional cruelty that Sadie found it difficult to wrap her mind around.

She gave Bryan one of their cheap slip leads since they had no idea what Brandon had done with Ivy's leash, and after thanking them a few more times, he left, taking the joyous dog with him, only to pop back into the lobby a few seconds later.

"Um, just so you know, there's someone in a Bigfoot costume in your parking lot."

Sadie let out a huff of laughter, while Penny gave him an incredulous look. She realized she had forgotten to tell her friend about the encounter with Kelsey.

"Thanks. Come on, Penny, we should go say hi."

They found Neil, Rory, and Kelsey outside, talking and joking as they packed their things into their vehicle. Kelsey seemed to be reenacting the moment she got hit by a car, which left the two young men roaring with laughter. Sadie waved at Bryan and Ivy as they drove away, then told the story to Penny in hushed tones. The trio of skunk ape enthusiasts hadn't been so bad, after all. While she doubted they would ever find what they were looking for, she wished them luck. Even if they didn't find the skunk ape, they certainly had a lot of fun looking for it.

It was a much-needed moment of happiness and peace after the chaos and stress of the past few days. In a few days, they would go to Joshua's funeral, but for now, Sadie was grateful for the chance to focus on what they had, rather than what they had lost.

Printed in Dunstable, United Kingdom